Pretzel and Pop's
Closetful of Stories

Pretzel and Pop's
CLOSETFUL of STORIES

by Jerry Smath

Silver Press

To Valerie, the real life Pretzel
J. S.

Published by Silver Press, a division of
Silver Burdett Press, Inc.
Simon & Schuster, Inc.
Prentice Hall Bldg., Englewood Cliffs, NJ 07632.
Printed in the United States of America.
10 9 8 7 6 5 4 3 2 1

Library of Congress Cataloging-in-Publication Data

Smath, Jerry.
  Pretzel and Pop's Closetful of stories/by Jerry Smath.
    p. cm.
  Summary: Pop tells Pretzel humorous stories about
various family members.
  [1. Family life—Fiction.   2. Fathers and daughters—
Fiction.   3. Rabbits—Fiction.   4. Humorous stories.]
  I. Title. PZ7.S6393Pr 1991
  [E]—dc20   90–8968
ISBN 0-671-72231-X (LSB)   CIP
ISBN 0-671-72232-8   AC

CONTENTS

Pretzel's pop sat reading

his newspaper.

He looked outside and saw Pretzel.

She was playing in the leaves.

"That looks like fun," said Pop.

"I think I will join her."

He went to the closet to get his hat.

But when he opened the closet door,
everything inside came tumbling out.
Pop was buried up to his whiskers
in toys and hats
and boxes and things.

7

Pretzel heard the noise.

She ran inside to see what

had happened.

"Oh, Pop, are you all right?"

asked Pretzel.

Pop shook his head.

"I am fine," he said,

"but I think it is time

to clean out the closet."

"I will help you," said Pretzel.

Together, they put almost

everything back.

But some things just did not fit.

"I can't throw away these things,"

said Pop.

"They remind me of family stories."

"Oh," Pretzel said with a smile.

"Please tell me the stories."

"All right," answered Pop.

Pretzel climbed into Pop's lap,

and he began the first story.

PRETZEL'S STICKY SHOE

One day Pretzel was late for school.

She kissed Pop goodbye

and ran out the door.

But she forgot her school bag.

On the way to school

Pretzel stepped on some gum.

The gum was pink and sticky.

It stuck to her shoe.

This made Pretzel angry.

But she kept on running.

As she ran along the road,

some leaves stuck to the gum.

Pretzel wanted to take off her shoe,

but she was late.

So she kept on running.

Then Pretzel stepped on

a twig and a piece of paper.

They stuck, too.

Pretzel shook her shoe hard.

But the leaf, the twig,

and the paper would not come off.

So she kept on going.

When Pretzel arrived at school,

the class had already begun.

Pretzel took her seat.

"Today, class, as you know,

we are having show-and-tell,"

said Miss Fox.

"What did you bring, Pretzel?"

"I brought my truck," Pretzel said.

"It is in my school bag."

Then, suddenly, Pretzel remembered.

"Oh, no!" she cried.

"I left my school bag at home!"

"Well, Pretzel,

do you have anything else to

show us?" asked Miss Fox.

Pretzel could not think of anything.

Then she looked down at her
sticky shoe.
"Yes, I do!" said Pretzel.
She took off the shoe
and carried it with her
as she hopped to the front
of the class.
Everyone laughed, especially Pretzel.

UNCLE JACK'S HAT

Uncle Jack was a magician,

but not a very good one.

One day, Aunt Dora bought him a hat.

"Maybe this will help," she said.

Uncle Jack put on the hat and

went to town to perform his magic.

17

A big crowd came to see his act.

"Pick a card," said Uncle Jack.

"I will tell you what it is."

A frog named Floretta picked a card.

"You picked a queen,"
Uncle Jack announced.
"Wrong," said Floretta.
"I have picked a king."
The crowd yelled, "Booooooo!"
but this did not stop Uncle Jack.
He took his bow anyway.

The next day,

as he was walking to town,

the wind blew Uncle Jack's hat off.

It went sailing into the woods.

Uncle Jack looked for it everywhere,

but he could not find it.

20

Then, suddenly, Uncle Jack looked up.

There, on a tree branch, was his hat.

A little bird had made it her home.

"What are you doing in my hat?"

demanded Uncle Jack.

The little bird looked sad.

"Do not make me go," said the bird.

"Your hat is the best home I ever had."

Uncle Jack felt sorry for the bird.

"Very well," he said. "You may stay.

But I will still wear my hat!"

With that, Uncle Jack went back to town

to do his magic act.

"Pick a card," said Uncle Jack.

A little mouse picked a card.

"You have picked a king,"

said Uncle Jack.

"I have not," said the mouse.

"I have picked a queen."

The crowd yelled, "Boooo!" again.

But that did not stop Uncle Jack.

He took his bow anyway,

and when he did . . .

. . . the bird flew out of his hat.
"Bravo!" everyone shouted,
and they all clapped for more.
They all clapped for Uncle Jack
and his magic hat.

AMAZING
JACK
THE
MAGICIAN

THE PUMPKIN PRINCESS

Halloween is a time to be scared

and be scary.

It is a time to dress up

and be silly.

Every year Pretzel and her cousin Corny

liked to spend Halloween together.

They liked to pretend to be witches

and goblins and even owls and bats.

"This year," said Pretzel,

"let's make our own costumes."

"That is a good idea!" said Corny.

"I will be a beautiful princess."

"And I will be a fat pumpkin,"

said Pretzel.

There was not much time.

Halloween was coming soon.

Corny started to sew her costume.

Pretzel started to make her mask.

But by the time Halloween arrived,

they were still busy working.

It was late afternoon

when they finally finished.

"How do you like my pumpkin mask?"

asked Pretzel.

"It is great!" said Corny.

"And how do you like my princess

costume?"

"It is beautiful," said Pretzel.

"Now we can go trick or treating."

Pretzel and Corny stepped outside.

A big harvest moon made spooky shadows

on the sidewalk.

From behind a tree

a green monster popped out.

"Hi, Corny," said the monster.

"How did you know it was me?"

asked Corny.

"You have no mask!" said the monster.

Corny and Pretzel

looked at each other.

"I forgot to make a mask!" said Corny.

"And I forgot to make a costume,"

said Pretzel.

Quickly, they both ran back

to Pretzel's house.

After a few minutes,

the front door slowly opened.

A tall, spooky creature with six arms

stepped onto the porch.

Ooooh! It was horrible!

It scared all the trick or treaters.

They were sure

THE PUMPKIN PRINCESS

FROM OUTER SPACE

had just landed in town!

POP'S VACUUM CLEANER

One day Pretzel and her pop
were cleaning the house.
Pretzel dusted,
while Pop used the vacuum cleaner.
Suddenly, the vacuum cleaner
stopped working.

"What happened?" asked Pretzel.

"I don't know," answered Pop.

"I will ask our neighbor,

Professor Harebrain, for help."

Pop called him on the telephone.

The professor came right over

and looked inside.

"Very interesting," he said,

"but if I were you,

this is what I would do . . ."

He pulled out some wheels

and put in some wires.

"I have fixed it,"

said Professor Harebrain.

He plugged in the vacuum cleaner.

Suddenly, it began to chase him.

Pretzel and Pop chased
the vacuum cleaner
that chased Professor Harebrain.

They chased it into the kitchen,

through the living room,

up the stairs,

down the stairs,

and back into the kitchen again.

36

Then the vacuum cleaner
spun around them in circles
and tied them all together.

Finally, Pop pulled out the plug,
and the vacuum cleaner stopped.

Professor Harebrain gave Pretzel

and Pop a funny little smile.

"Very interesting," he said,

"but if I were you,

this is what I would do . . .

I would buy a new vacuum cleaner!"

AUNT DORA'S DRUM

Aunt Dora was bored.

"I wish I had a hobby," she said.

"Playing music might be nice,"

said Uncle Jack.

Aunt Dora liked the idea.

So she put on her coat

and went to the music store.

Later, Aunt Dora came back with

a little drum.

She started beating the drum

right away.

"The sooner I practice,

the sooner I will learn to play,"

Aunt Dora said.

Ratta-tat-tat. Ratta-tat-tat.

Aunt Dora played all morning.

Ratta-tat-tat. Ratta-tat-tat.

Aunt Dora played all night.

Then she played,

Ratta-tat-tat-tat-tat.

"Did you hear that, Jack?"

she asked.

"I am getting much better,

don't you agree?"

Uncle Jack did not say a word.

He just held his ears.

Every day

Aunt Dora played her drum.

Ratta-tat-tat. Ratta-tat-tat.

Her neighbor, Mr. Owl, called

on the telephone to complain.

Aunt Dora just shut the windows

and kept on playing.

Ratta-tat-tat. Ratta-tat-tat.

One day, Mrs. Mole rang the doorbell

to complain about the noise.

Aunt Dora took her drum

to the attic,

but she kept on playing.

Ratta-tat-tat. Ratta-tat-tat.

Uncle Jack did not want to hurt
Aunt Dora's feelings.
"I am glad you have a hobby," he said.
"But maybe that little drum
is not quite right for you."
Aunt Dora agreed with him.
She stopped playing the little drum
and went back to the music store.
At last the house was quiet.
Uncle Jack sat down and read his book.

When Aunt Dora came back,

she was dragging a big bass drum.

"You were right!" she said.

"That *little* drum was not right for me.

So I bought a bigger one!"

BOOM! BOOM! BOOM! she played.

Uncle Jack went for a long walk.

UNCLE BENNY'S VISIT

Uncle Benny arrived for a visit.

He had quit his job driving

the garbage truck

and now he had nothing to do.

"Why not help out around our house?"

Pop and Pretzel suggested.

47

Pretzel's grandmother was in the kitchen

making a chocolate cake.

Uncle Benny wanted to help her.

"I will mix the cake batter," he said.

But Uncle Benny was not sure

which button to push on the mixer.

So he pushed all of them.

The batter went flying everywhere.

Poor Grandma was so upset!

Uncle Benny felt terrible.

"I guess I'm not
a very good baker,"
Uncle Benny said.
Then he went outside.

Pop was painting the house.

Uncle Benny wanted to help,

so he climbed the ladder.

But the ladder started to shake.

Pop lost his balance.

Uncle Benny felt bad.

"I guess I'm not a very good

house painter, either," he sighed.

Uncle Benny sat down beside Pretzel.

She was playing with her toy truck.

"I once drove a big truck like that,"

Uncle Benny said to Pretzel.

"And I was good at it, too!

I wish I had never quit that job."

"Tell me about it," said Pretzel.

But just as he was about to begin,

a real garbage truck came by.

The workers on the truck

called out to Uncle Benny.

"We need your help!

Please come back to work with us."

Uncle Benny did not have to think twice!

He got in the truck and,

with a smile on his face,

he waved goodbye to Pretzel and Pop.

Then he drove off to work.

PROFESSOR HAREBRAIN'S SURPRISE

To Pretzel.
from
Prof. Harebrain

It was Pretzel's birthday.

Pop gave her a big birthday party.

Grandma gave her running shoes.

Aunt Dora and Uncle Jack

gave Pretzel a shiny trumpet.

Cousin Corny and Uncle Benny

gave her a toy truck.

Professor Harebrain could not come,

but he sent her a present.

Pop helped Pretzel open the box.

Everyone gathered around.

"What an odd-looking thing,"
said Pop.

"I wonder what it is," said Pretzel.

"I know what it is,"

said Grandma.

"It is a cake mixer."

She tried to use it,

but it did not work.

"No!" said Aunt Dora.

"I know what it is.

It is a musical instrument."

She tried to play it,
but no sound came out.
"You are both wrong,"
said Uncle Jack.
"This is a magic-trick machine."
He waved his magic wand over it,
but nothing happened.

Then Cousin Corny picked it up.

"It is a spaceship," she said.

She tried to launch it,

but it did not blast-off.

Uncle Benny just said,

"It looks like junk to me."

Pretzel saw that

the strange-looking thing

had a button on the top.

She bent down and pushed the button.

Professor Harebrain's present
lit up and moved.
Bubbles blew and flags waved.
The machine sputtered
and scooted around the room.

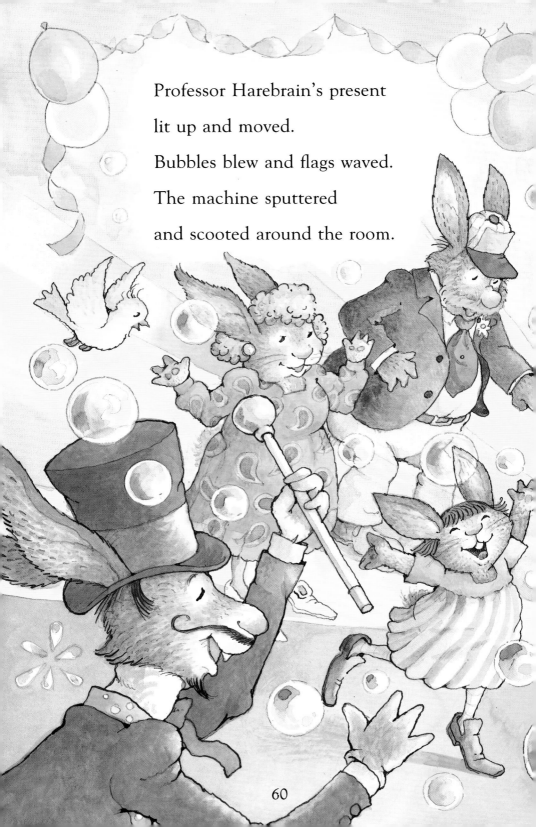

Suddenly, the top flew open
and a toy bunny popped out
with a sign that said:

HAPPY BIRTHDAY PRETZEL!

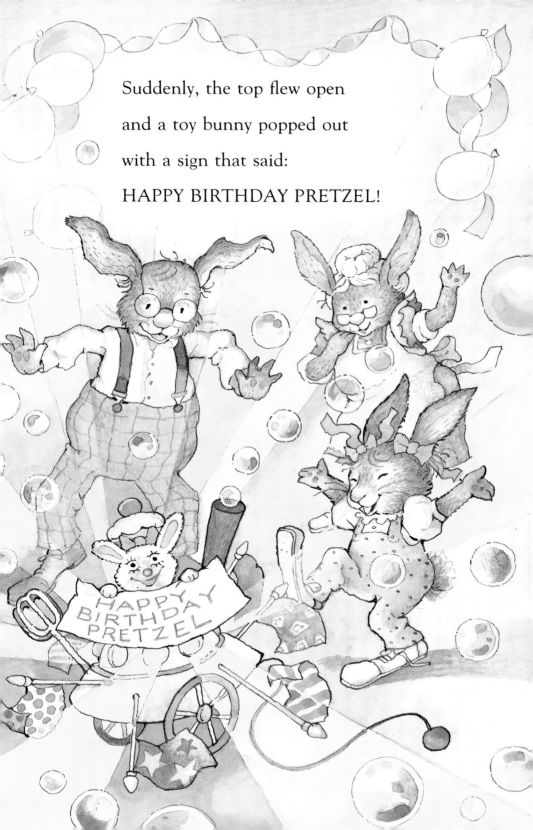

When Pop finished telling his stories

Pretzel gave him a big hug.

Then she helped Pop stuff

the rest of the things

back into the closet.

"I am glad you did not throw
anything away," said Pretzel.
"Me, too," said Pop.
Then they both went out to play.